CELESTINA
the Astronaut Ballerina

Donald Jacobsen

Illustrations by
Graham Evans

GIBBS SMITH
TO ENRICH AND INSPIRE HUMANKIND

When Celestina was a little girl,
her dreams were big—they were out of this world!
She did not want to be an athlete,
to be a star, or to work on Wall Street.

No, she had bigger plans than that,
and those plans came with a special hat.
She truly wanted to walk and explore
where no little girl had set foot before.

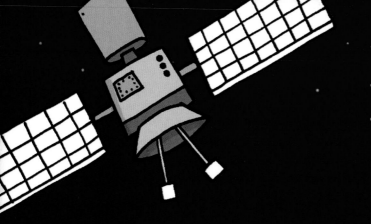

The dream that she dreamed was to walk on the moon!
And she could not leave a minute too soon.
She would go in a rocket and fly into space,
and be the first little girl to visit that place.

But to fly to the moon, you first have to train.
You have to work hard—that's simple and plain.
You need to be smart to pass every test.
There's no doubt about it, you must be the best!

And Celestina surely tried her best
to fulfill her mission and finish her quest.
But every time this young dreamer spoke,
the other kids laughed and made her feel like a joke.

All through school, before, even after,
the kids would jeer and burst out in laughter.
They mocked Celestina for the dream that she had,
and all of their teasing made her feel really sad.

And what of adults? What did they have to say?
Did they tell Celestina her dream was okay?
No. All the grown-ups, they fussed and they mumbled,
they carped, and they griped, and they whined, and
they grumbled.

"Celestina," they told her, in stern and harsh voices,
"This path is too hard—you must think of your choices.
Being an astronaut is thrilling and grand,
but it takes too much work! You need a much better plan."

"Come on, Celestina, it's time now to change,
and to think of things that are not quite so strange."
Her teacher then said to sweet Celestina,
"You, my dear, would make a great ballerina."

"I do love to dance and twirl, it's true,
but I can be an astronaut, too!"
Celestina's words about her dreams fell short.
Her teacher laughed with a big, rude snort.

So she traded away the stars at night
for pointed slippers and a pair of pink tights.
She left behind her cool rocket jet
and learned to do a smooth pirouette.

She placed her feet in first position,
and forgot about her heartfelt mission.
Her dream to travel and fly through space
disappeared without a single trace.

TOYS

GALAXY

She practiced hard; she practiced long.
Her feet became tough, her muscles strong.
Celestina could dance, and oh, she could spin!
But something was not right within.

She was not happy, no, not completely,
even though Celestina could dance so sweetly.
When she jumped up, she floated so high.
But still, she dreamed of conquering the sky.

She shook the thought right out of her head.
She tried not to think of it, lying in bed.
She did not talk about space anymore.
She was not the same girl she had been before.

But then one day a new teacher came.
Miss Stella, they said, was this woman's name.
Maybe she was not like the rest.
What happened next, you wouldn't have guessed . . .

"What are each of your dreams and your desires?
What are the things to which you aspire?"
Miss Stella asked every boy, every girl,
"What is your biggest, brightest hope in the world?"

Celestina was shocked; this surprised the young girl.
She liked this smart teacher who seemed out of this world.
Instead of them telling her what she should be,
Celestina could choose; her way was now free!

"To be a ballerina is a great ambition,
but, Miss Stella, I do not think that's my mission.
For years, I've been thinking a much bigger thought:
That I really should be an astronaut."

"Well," said Miss Stella, "it's time that you soar.
Trade in your ballet shoes for the great rocket's roar.
Dream your big dreams and never give in.
It is never too late for you to begin."

Celestina was inspired and then filled with hope.
She graduated college, but did she stop there? Nope!
When she finished school, off to NASA she went,
and many years in training and learning she spent.

She learned about launches and landings and more.
There were so many subjects for her to explore!
She often felt tired after all of her training.
But she did it all without ever complaining.

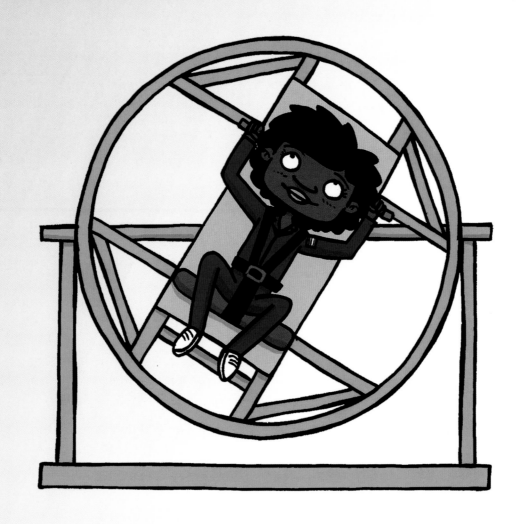

And after all that, she was part of a team.
Through all of that effort, she was living her dream.
But when it came time to fly to the moon,
her commander instead sang a different tune.

Her great lunar mission had to be cut a bit short,
and traded for one of a different sort.
Celestina smiled and looked up at the stars.
Her new stellar mission was to walk upon Mars!

For 200 days in a rocket, she flew.
She followed her dreams and led her new crew.
She waved to the moon as they zoomed on by.
The best way to travel was surely to fly.

And 200 days after leaving the Earth,
she finally knew how much she was worth.
A spark from Miss Stella had grown and grown.
Celestina had made her dreams her own.

As the brave astronauts rocketed down,
they landed on Mars with a roaring sound.
They knew they would see the mission through,
with their great Celestina leading the crew.

With confidence, Celestina stepped out onto Mars.
With wonder, Celestina looked out at the stars.
And on that red planet, our great Celestina
danced like a brilliant astronaut ballerina.

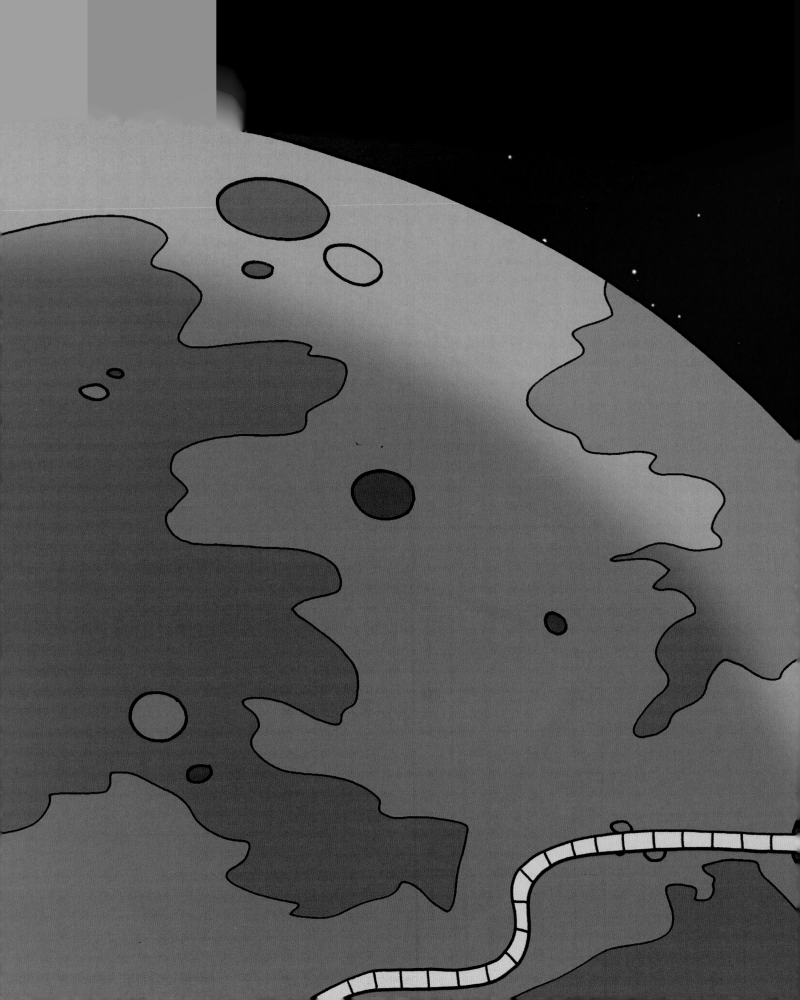

The end.

To Meemaw, who taught me how to fly.

"Loved this and wish I'd read it as a girl. Rhyming is stellar.
Story fresh and fantastic. I loved it!" —Pam Darbonne

"This is a book of dreams. The little ones will love knowing that
they can literally dream for the stars. The illustrations are beautiful
and the storyline is new and exciting." —Cynthia Gutzwiller

"This book is wonderful. The words, illustrations and message are all beautiful.
My daughter has asked to read this one every night!" —Jessica Mack

"The illustrations are beautiful and the message is an important one for children:
Have your dreams and don't be afraid to reach for them." —Deanie Humphrys-Dunne

"Beautifully written, a fantastic moral and amazing
illustrations, this book has it all." —Lieve Snellings

First Edition
25 24 23 22 21   5 4 3 2 1

Text and Illustrations © 2021 Donald Jacobsen
Illustrations by Graham Evans

All rights reserved. No part of this book may be
reproduced by any means whatsoever without written
permission from the publisher, except brief portions
quoted for purpose of review.

Published by
Gibbs Smith
P.O. Box 667
Layton, Utah 84041

1.800.835.4993 orders
www.gibbs-smith.com

Manufactured in Shenzhen, China, in January 2021 by
Toppan Printing

Gibbs Smith books are printed on either recycled,
100% post-consumer waste, FSC-certified papers or on
paper produced from sustainable PEFC-certified forest/
controlled wood source. Learn more at www.pefc.org.

Library of Congress Control Number: 2020941754
ISBN: 978-1-4236-5680-7